THIS CANDLEWICK BOOK BELONGS TO:

_____

_____

_____

_____

For my mother and father

*I would like to thank Helen Read for the
decorative borders she designed and
painted so beautifully.*

F.M.

The Honey Hunters is an adaptation of a traditional tale
told by the Ngoni people of Africa.

This retelling is based on "The Quarrel" © 1939 by Geraldine Elliott from
The Long Grass Whispers, published by Routledge & Kegan Paul, Ltd.

First U.S. paperback edition 1994
First published in Great Britain in 1992 by
Walker Books Ltd., London.

Library of Congress Cataloging-in-Publication Data

Martin, Francesca.
The honey hunters / by Francesca Martin.
Summary: An African folktale in which various animals peacefully follow a
honey guide bird, but find that sharing the honey among themselves causes problems.
ISBN 1-56402-086-X (hardcover)
[1. Folklore—Africa.   2. Animals—Folklore.]   I. Title.
PZ8.1.M368Ho   1992
398.24'52'096—dc20   91-58736
ISBN 1-56402-276-5 (paperback)

10 9 8 7 6 5 4 3 2 1

Printed in Hong Kong

The pictures in this book were done in watercolor.

Candlewick Press
2067 Massachusetts Avenue
Cambridge, Massachusetts 02140

The Honey Hunters

A traditional African tale illustrated by
Francesca Martin

CANDLEWICK PRESS
CAMBRIDGE, MASSACHUSETTS

Once upon a time, all the wild animals were the greatest of friends. And, as it happened, they all loved honey. The little gray honey guide knew the best places to find honey. "Che, che! Cheka, cheka, che!" the bird would cry. "If you want honey, follow me!"

One day a boy was walking by the lake
when he heard the honey guide's song.
"I'd like some honey," he said. "I'll follow you."
And so the boy and the honey guide set off
together through the bush.

Soon they met a rooster.

"Che, che! Cheka, cheka, che!" sang the
honey guide. "If you want honey, follow me!"

"I'd like some honey," said the rooster, fluffing
up his tail feathers. "I'll follow you."

And so the rooster joined the boy as he followed
the honey guide through the bush.

They had not gone far
when they saw a bush cat.
"Che, che! Cheka, cheka, che!" sang the
honey guide. "If you want honey, follow me!"
"I'd like some honey," said the bush cat,
dropping from the tree. "I'll follow you."
So the honey guide and the boy and the rooster
and the bush cat set off together.

By and by they met an antelope . . .   and then a leopard . . .   and then a zebra . . .

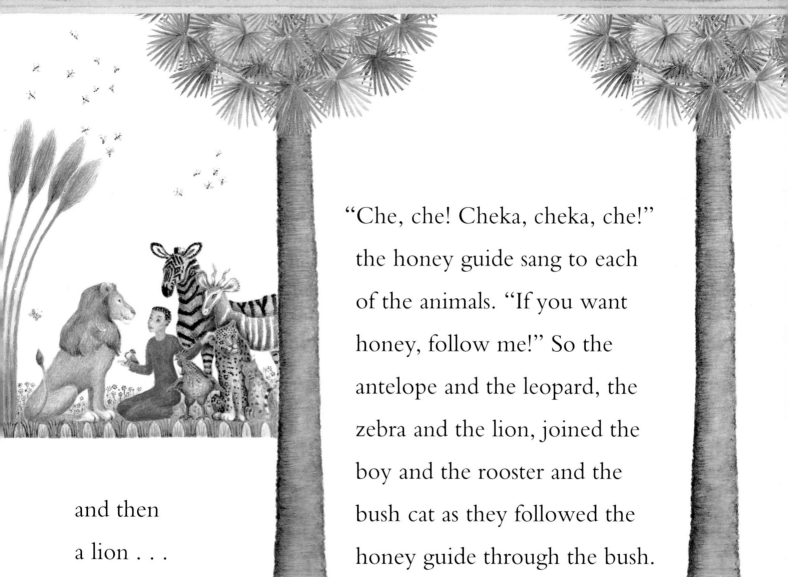

and then
a lion . . .

"Che, che! Cheka, cheka, che!" the honey guide sang to each of the animals. "If you want honey, follow me!" So the antelope and the leopard, the zebra and the lion, joined the boy and the rooster and the bush cat as they followed the honey guide through the bush.

Soon the animals met an elephant.

"Where are you all going, my friends?" he asked.

"To find some honey," replied the boy.

"Che, che! Cheka, cheka, che!" sang the honey guide.

"If you want honey, follow me!"

So the elephant joined the procession
of animals going in search of honey.

In a short while, the honey guide stopped.

"Che, che! Cheka, cheka, che!" he sang again.

"If you want honey, look in this tree!"

Then the boy took a beautiful honeycomb

from the bees' nest and broke it into four pieces.

The first he gave to the rooster and the bush cat.

The second he gave to the antelope and the leopard.

The third he gave to the zebra and the lion.

And the fourth he kept for himself and the elephant.

Then all the animals began to eat . . .

The rooster pecked his
end of the honeycomb
and the bush cat licked his.
Then the bush cat spat at
the rooster and the rooster
scratched the bush cat.

The antelope nibbled her
end of the honeycomb
and the leopard gulped his.
Then the leopard clawed the
antelope and the antelope
kicked the leopard.

The zebra chewed her end
of the honeycomb and the
lion tore off a big chunk.
Then the lion leapt upon the
zebra and the zebra bit the
lion with her sharp teeth.

The elephant seized the
honeycomb from the boy
and swallowed it whole.
And the boy just stared
in amazement at the
squabbling animals.

"Stop!" the boy cried. "Don't fight!

You have never quarreled with each other before!"

But the animals refused to listen.

In desperation the boy picked up a stick

and waved it at them.

At this, the animals fell silent.

The elephant turned to the boy and said sadly,

"The damage is done. We can never be friends again.

From now on, the rooster will fight the bush cat,

the antelope will fight the leopard, the zebra will

fight the lion, and I will fight you and all your kind."

But the honey guide still sat peacefully on the boy's hand, and near them in the bush were many other animals—the squirrel and the porcupine, the owl and the mouse, the snake and the butterfly, the beetle and the snail. "Che, che! Cheka, cheka, che!" sang the honey guide. "If you want honey, follow me."

FRANCESCA MARTIN was born in Kenya, where she lived until she was sixteen years old. She later studied design in college, and now does free-lance design and architectural drawing. Francesca Martin remembered this tale of the honey hunter from a collection of stories she was given as a child. She has illustrated one other picture book for children, *Lottie's Cats*.